THE MARVELOUS LAND OF OZ

VOL. 2

ADAPTED FROM THE NOVEL BY L. FRANK BAUM

Writer: **ERIC SHANOWER**
Artist: **SKOTTIE YOUNG**
Colorist: **JEAN-FRANCOIS BEAULIEU**
Letterer: **JEFF ECKLEBERRY**

Assistant Editor: **MICHAEL HORWITZ**
Editor: **NATE COSBY**

Collection Editor: **MARK D. BEAZLEY**
Assistant Editors: **ALEX STARBUCK & NELSON RIBEIRO**
Editor, Special Projects: **JENNIFER GRÜNWALD**
Senior Editor, Special Projects: **JEFF YOUNGQUIST**
SVP of Print & Digital Publishing Sales: **DAVID GABRIEL**
Production: **JERRY KALINOWSKI**
Book Design: **ARLENE SO**

Editor in Chief: **AXEL ALONSO**
Chief Creative Officer: **JOE QUESADA**
Publisher: **DAN BUCKLEY**
Executive Producer: **ALAN FINE**

MARVEL

visit us at www.abdopublishing.com

Reinforced library bound edition published in 2014 by Spotlight, a division of the ABDO Group, PO Box 398166, Minneapolis, Minnesota 55439. Spotlight produces high-quality reinforced library bound editions for schools and libraries. Published by agreement with Marvel Characters, Inc.

Printed in the United States of America, North Mankato, Minnesota.
102013
012014
This book contains at least 10% recycled materials.

Marvel.com
© 2014 Marvel

Library of Congress Cataloging-in-Publication Data

Shanower, Eric.
  The marvelous land of Oz / adapted from the novel by L. Frank Baum ; writer: Eric Shanower ; artist: Skottie Young. -- Reinforced library bound edition.
      pages cm
  "Marvel."
  Summary: When the Scarecrow, now the ruler of the Emerald City, is driven out by General Jinjur and her all-girl army, his friends--the Tin Woodman, a boy named Tip, and Jack Pumpkinhead--try to restore peace in this graphic novel adaptation of L. Frank Baum's classic tale.
  ISBN 978-1-61479-235-2 (vol. 1) -- ISBN 978-1-61479-236-9 (vol. 2) -- ISBN 978-1-61479-237-6 (vol. 3) -- ISBN 978-1-61479-238-3 (vol. 4) -- ISBN 978-1-61479-239-0 (vol. 5) -- ISBN 978-1-61479-240-6 (vol. 6) -- ISBN 978-1-61479-241-3 (vol. 7) -- ISBN 978-1-61479-242-0 (vol. 8)
  1. Graphic novels. [1. Graphic novels. 2. Fantasy.] I. Young, Skottie, illustrator. II. Baum, L. Frank (Lyman Frank), 1856-1919. Marvelous land of Oz. III. Title.
  PZ7.7.S453Mar 2014
  741.5'973--dc23
                                        2013030127

All Spotlight books are reinforced library binding
and manufactured in the United States of America.

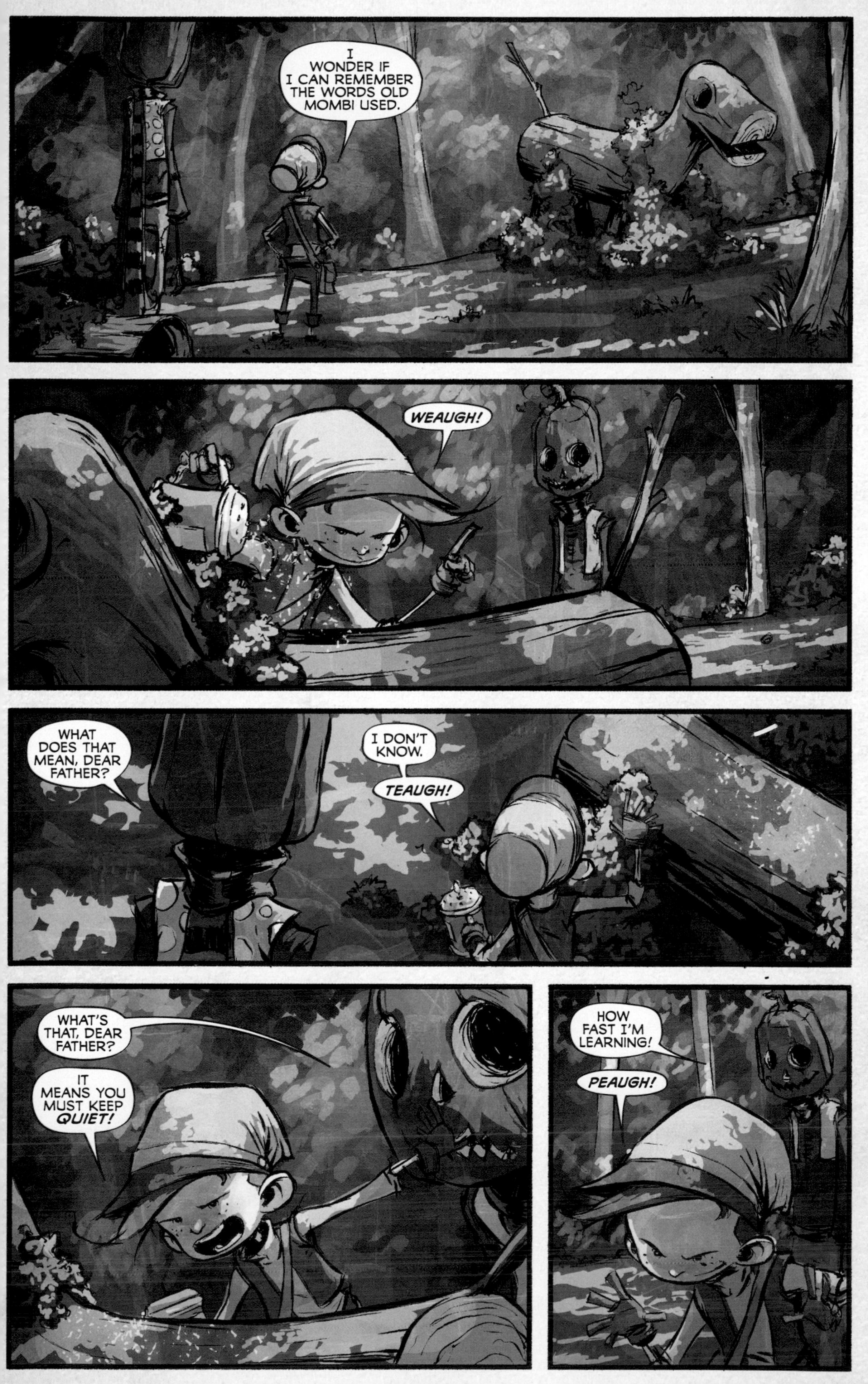
I WONDER IF I CAN REMEMBER THE WORDS OLD MOMBI USED.
WEAUGH!
WHAT DOES THAT MEAN, DEAR FATHER?
I DON'T KNOW.
TEAUGH!
WHAT'S THAT, DEAR FATHER?
IT MEANS YOU MUST KEEP *QUIET!*
HOW FAST I'M LEARNING!
PEAUGH!

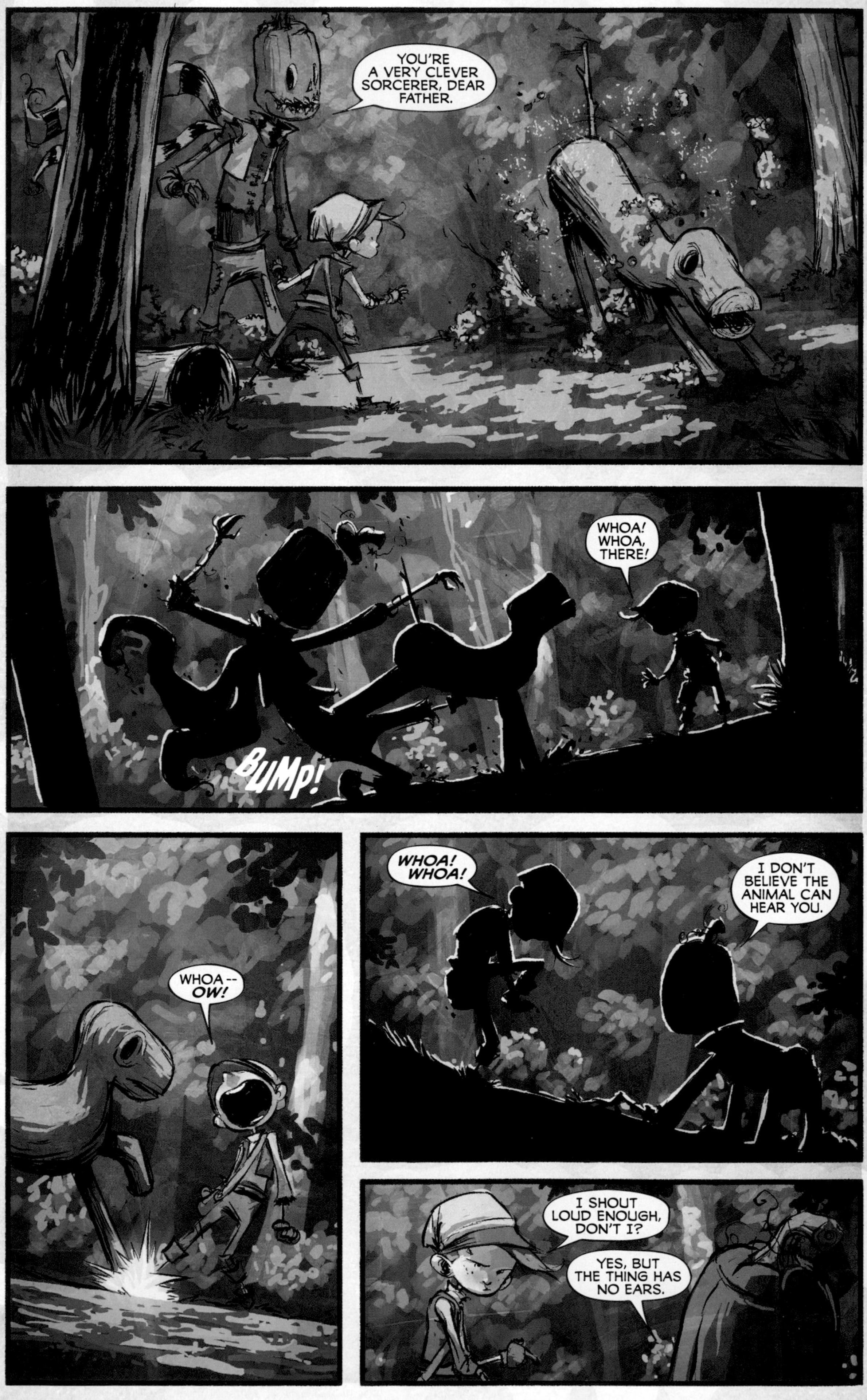

YOU'RE A VERY CLEVER SORCERER, DEAR FATHER.
WHOA! WHOA, THERE!
BUMP!
WHOA -- OW!
WHOA! WHOA!
I DON'T BELIEVE THE ANIMAL CAN HEAR YOU.
I SHOUT LOUD ENOUGH, DON'T I?
YES, BUT THE THING HAS NO EARS.

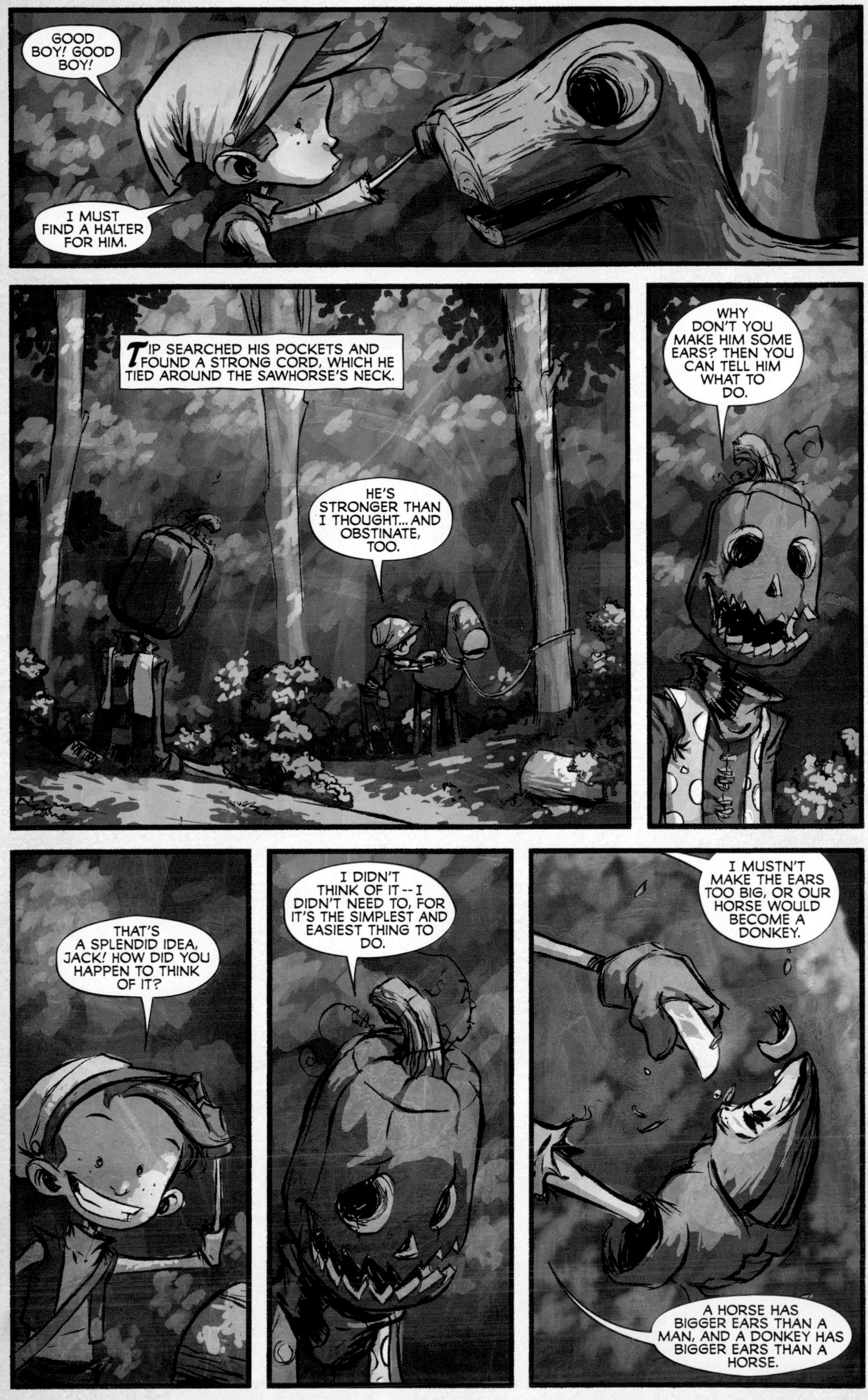
GOOD BOY! GOOD BOY!
I MUST FIND A HALTER FOR HIM.
TIP SEARCHED HIS POCKETS AND FOUND A STRONG CORD, WHICH HE TIED AROUND THE SAWHORSE'S NECK.
HE'S STRONGER THAN I THOUGHT... AND OBSTINATE, TOO.
WHY DON'T YOU MAKE HIM SOME EARS? THEN YOU CAN TELL HIM WHAT TO DO.
THAT'S A SPLENDID IDEA, JACK! HOW DID YOU HAPPEN TO THINK OF IT?
I DIDN'T THINK OF IT -- I DIDN'T NEED TO, FOR IT'S THE SIMPLEST AND EASIEST THING TO DO.
I MUSTN'T MAKE THE EARS TOO BIG, OR OUR HORSE WOULD BECOME A DONKEY.
A HORSE HAS BIGGER EARS THAN A MAN, AND A DONKEY HAS BIGGER EARS THAN A HORSE.

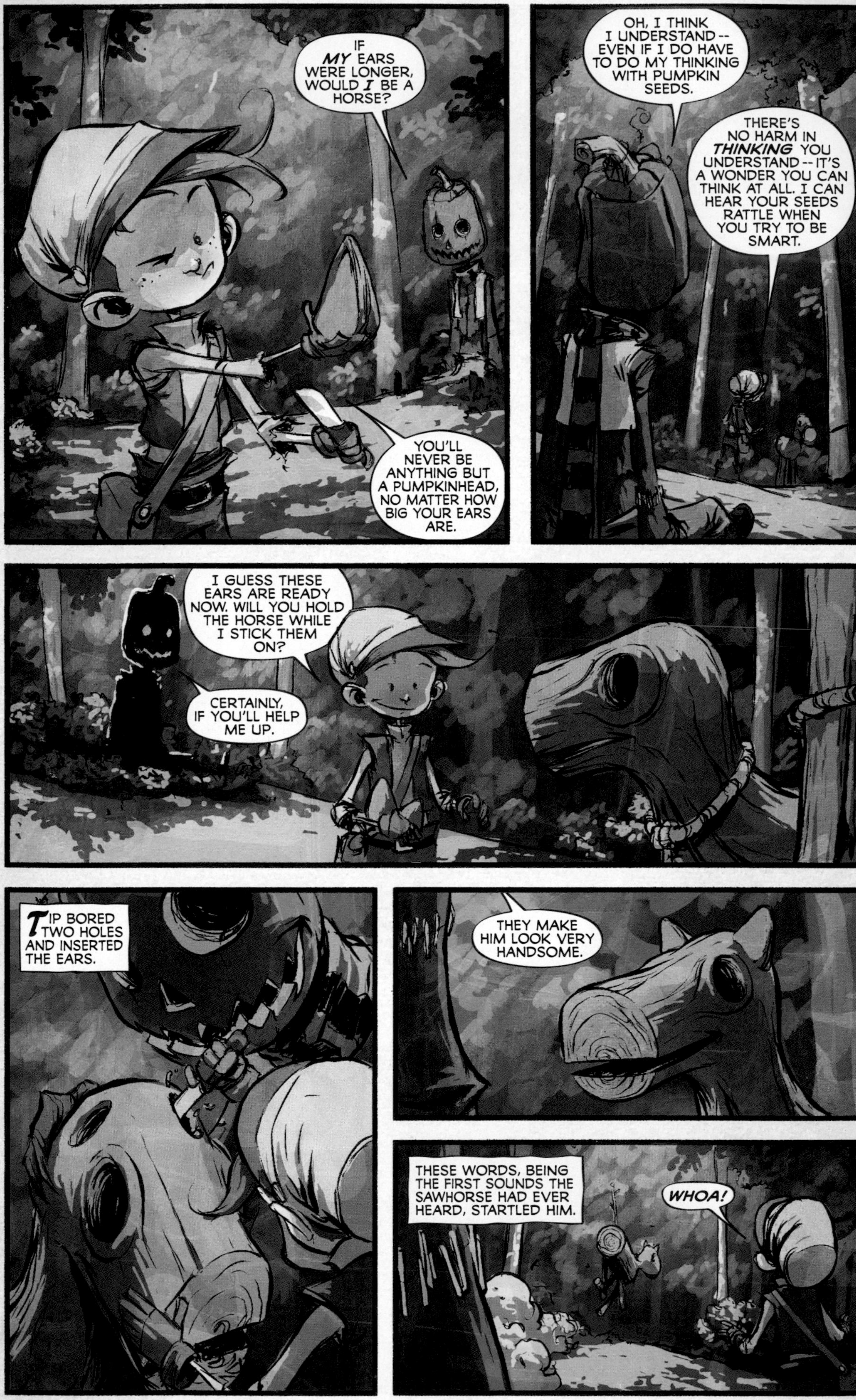
IF MY EARS WERE LONGER, WOULD I BE A HORSE?
YOU'LL NEVER BE ANYTHING BUT A PUMPKINHEAD, NO MATTER HOW BIG YOUR EARS ARE.
OH, I THINK I UNDERSTAND -- EVEN IF I DO HAVE TO DO MY THINKING WITH PUMPKIN SEEDS.
THERE'S NO HARM IN THINKING YOU UNDERSTAND -- IT'S A WONDER YOU CAN THINK AT ALL. I CAN HEAR YOUR SEEDS RATTLE WHEN YOU TRY TO BE SMART.
I GUESS THESE EARS ARE READY NOW. WILL YOU HOLD THE HORSE WHILE I STICK THEM ON?
CERTAINLY, IF YOU'LL HELP ME UP.
TIP BORED TWO HOLES AND INSERTED THE EARS.
THEY MAKE HIM LOOK VERY HANDSOME.
THESE WORDS, BEING THE FIRST SOUNDS THE SAWHORSE HAD EVER HEARD, STARTLED HIM.
WHOA!

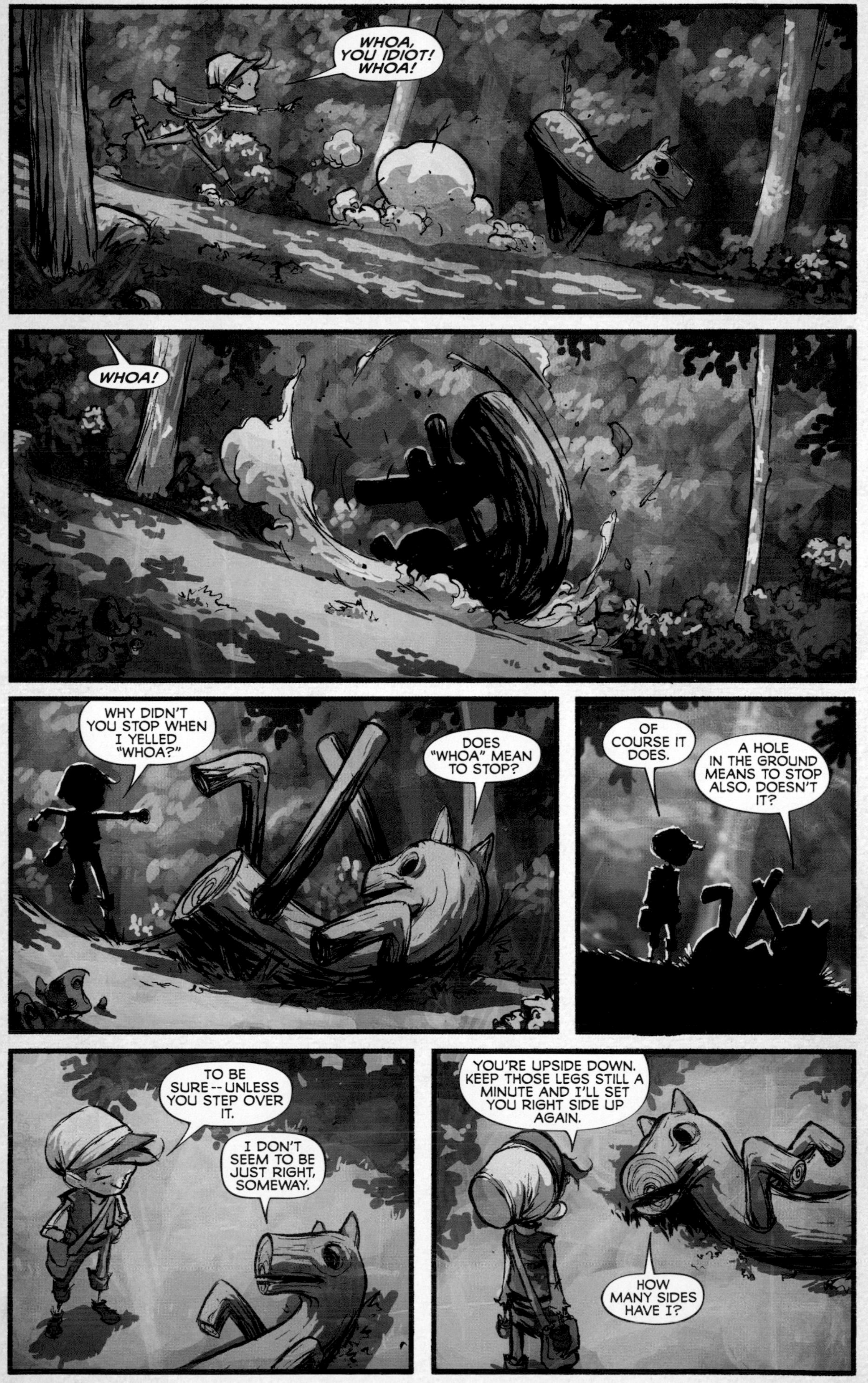
WHOA, YOU IDIOT! WHOA!
WHOA!
WHY DIDN'T YOU STOP WHEN I YELLED "WHOA?"
DOES "WHOA" MEAN TO STOP?
OF COURSE IT DOES.
A HOLE IN THE GROUND MEANS TO STOP ALSO, DOESN'T IT?
TO BE SURE--UNLESS YOU STEP OVER IT.
I DON'T SEEM TO BE JUST RIGHT, SOMEWAY.
YOU'RE UPSIDE DOWN. KEEP THOSE LEGS STILL A MINUTE AND I'LL SET YOU RIGHT SIDE UP AGAIN.
HOW MANY SIDES HAVE I?

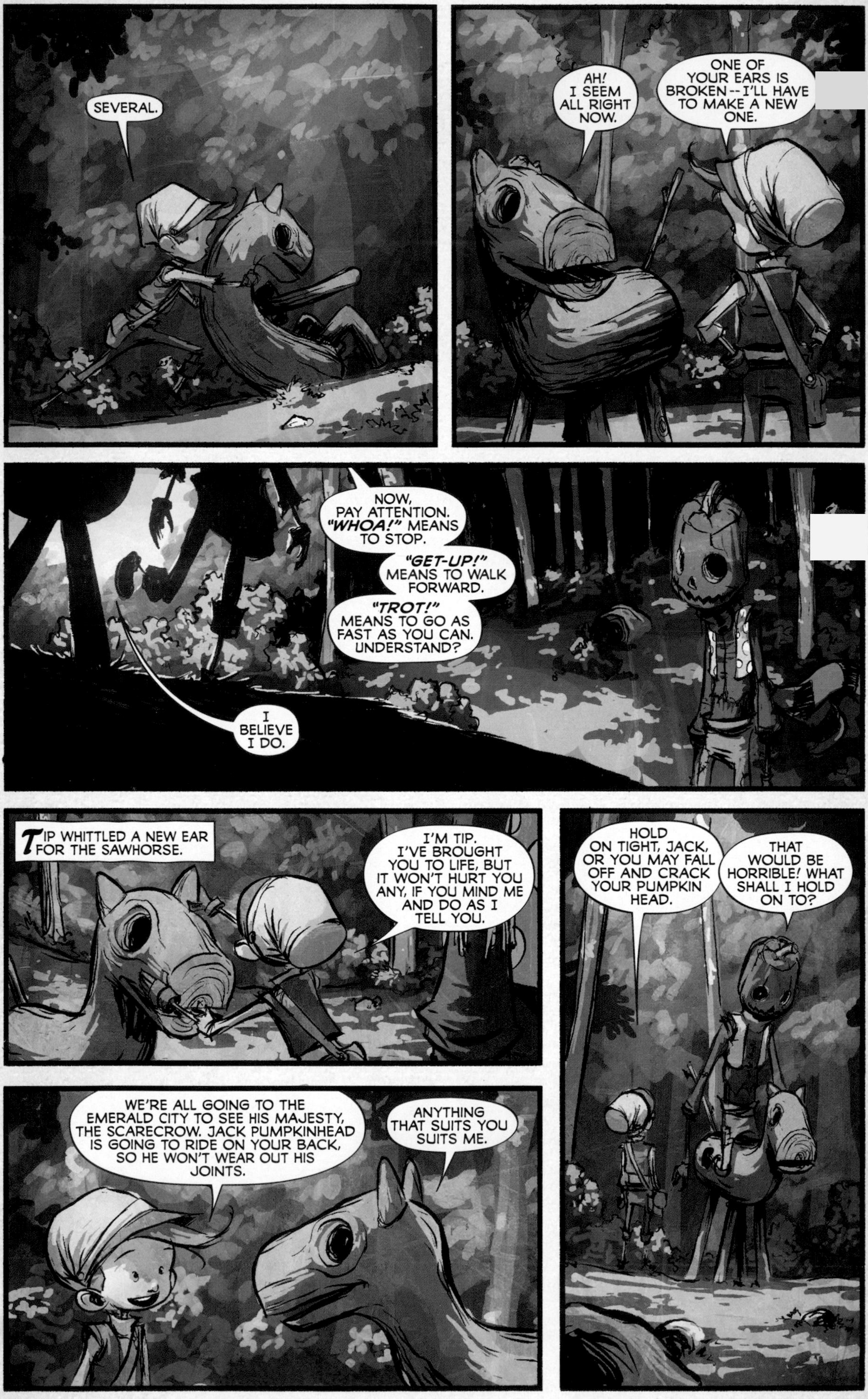
SEVERAL.
AH! I SEEM ALL RIGHT NOW.
ONE OF YOUR EARS IS BROKEN -- I'LL HAVE TO MAKE A NEW ONE.
NOW, PAY ATTENTION. "WHOA!" MEANS TO STOP.
"GET-UP!" MEANS TO WALK FORWARD.
"TROT!" MEANS TO GO AS FAST AS YOU CAN. UNDERSTAND?
I BELIEVE I DO.
TIP WHITTLED A NEW EAR FOR THE SAWHORSE.
I'M TIP. I'VE BROUGHT YOU TO LIFE, BUT IT WON'T HURT YOU ANY, IF YOU MIND ME AND DO AS I TELL YOU.
WE'RE ALL GOING TO THE EMERALD CITY TO SEE HIS MAJESTY, THE SCARECROW. JACK PUMPKINHEAD IS GOING TO RIDE ON YOUR BACK, SO HE WON'T WEAR OUT HIS JOINTS.
ANYTHING THAT SUITS YOU SUITS ME.
HOLD ON TIGHT, JACK, OR YOU MAY FALL OFF AND CRACK YOUR PUMPKIN HEAD.
THAT WOULD BE HORRIBLE! WHAT SHALL I HOLD ON TO?

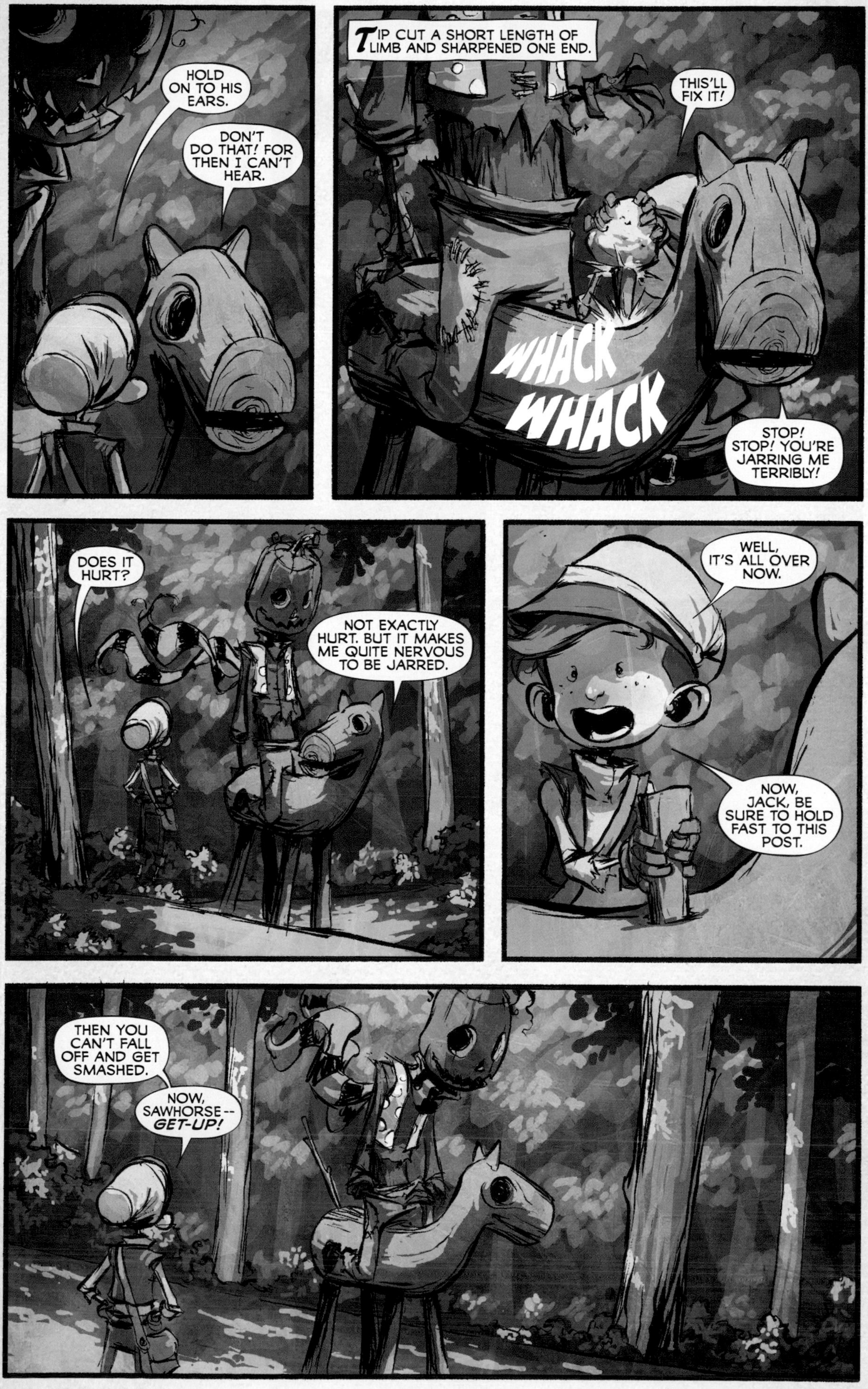
HOLD ON TO HIS EARS.
DON'T DO THAT! FOR THEN I CAN'T HEAR.
TIP CUT A SHORT LENGTH OF LIMB AND SHARPENED ONE END.
THIS'LL FIX IT!
WHACK
WHACK
STOP! STOP! YOU'RE JARRING ME TERRIBLY!
DOES IT HURT?
NOT EXACTLY HURT. BUT IT MAKES ME QUITE NERVOUS TO BE JARRED.
WELL, IT'S ALL OVER NOW.
NOW, JACK, BE SURE TO HOLD FAST TO THIS POST.
THEN YOU CAN'T FALL OFF AND GET SMASHED.
NOW, SAWHORSE-- GET-UP!

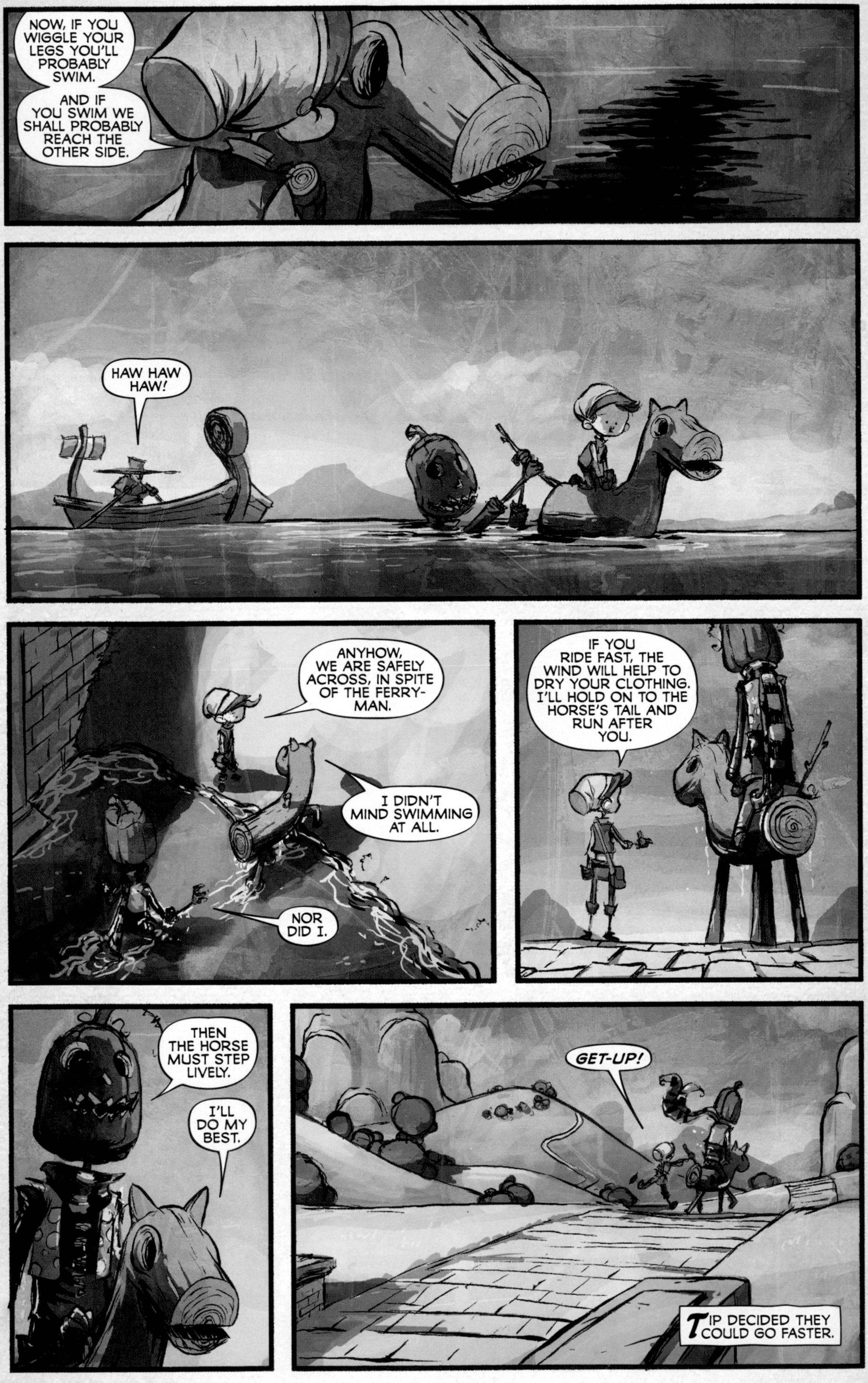
NOW, IF YOU WIGGLE YOUR LEGS YOU'LL PROBABLY SWIM.
AND IF YOU SWIM WE SHALL PROBABLY REACH THE OTHER SIDE.
HAW HAW HAW!
ANYHOW, WE ARE SAFELY ACROSS, IN SPITE OF THE FERRY-MAN.
I DIDN'T MIND SWIMMING AT ALL.
NOR DID I.
IF YOU RIDE FAST, THE WIND WILL HELP TO DRY YOUR CLOTHING. I'LL HOLD ON TO THE HORSE'S TAIL AND RUN AFTER YOU.
THEN THE HORSE MUST STEP LIVELY.
I'LL DO MY BEST.
GET-UP!
TIP DECIDED THEY COULD GO FASTER.

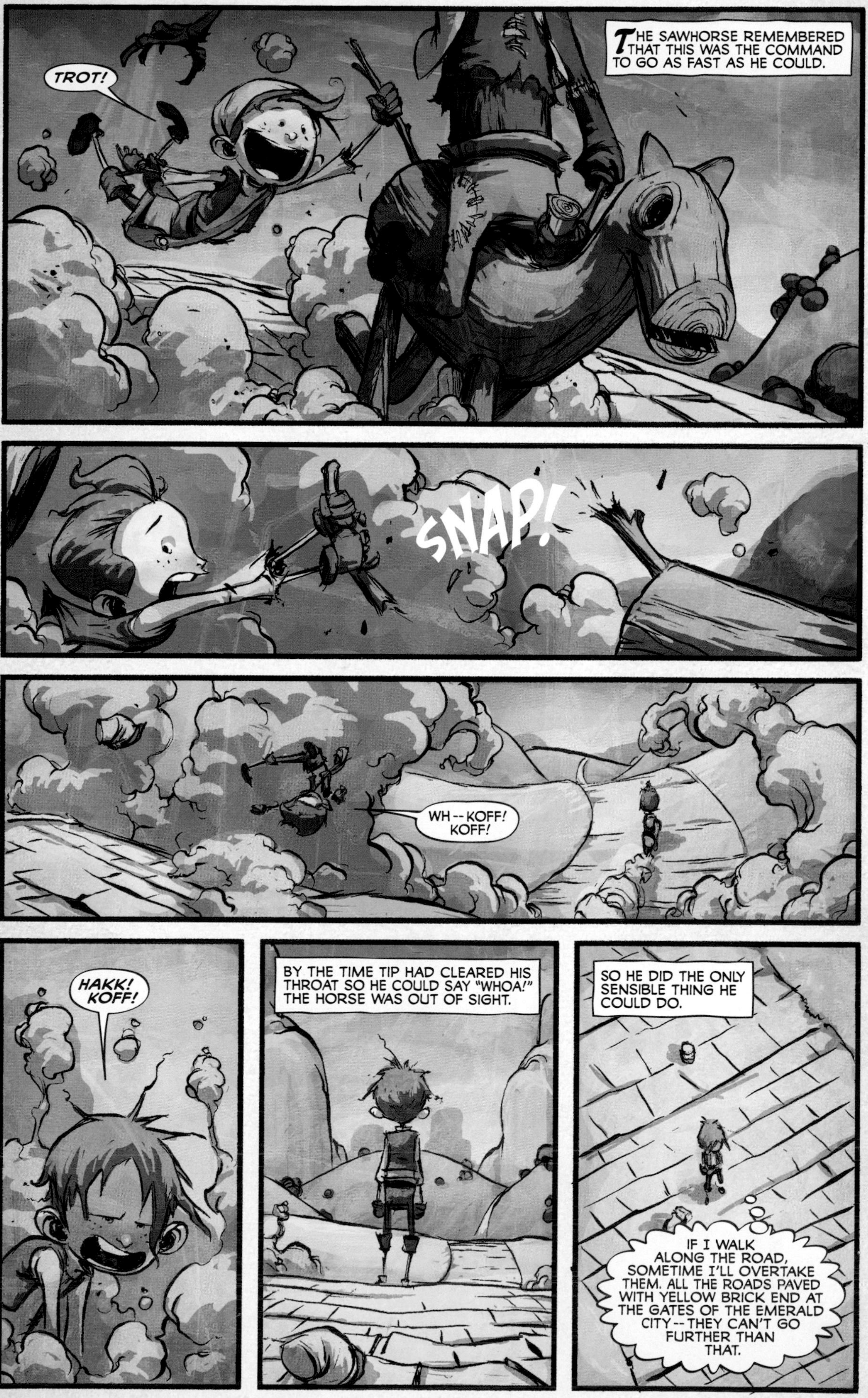
THE SAWHORSE REMEMBERED THAT THIS WAS THE COMMAND TO GO AS FAST AS HE COULD.
TROT!
SNAP!
WH--KOFF! KOFF!
HAKK! KOFF!
BY THE TIME TIP HAD CLEARED HIS THROAT SO HE COULD SAY "WHOA!" THE HORSE WAS OUT OF SIGHT.
SO HE DID THE ONLY SENSIBLE THING HE COULD DO.
IF I WALK ALONG THE ROAD, SOMETIME I'LL OVERTAKE THEM. ALL THE ROADS PAVED WITH YELLOW BRICK END AT THE GATES OF THE EMERALD CITY--THEY CAN'T GO FURTHER THAN THAT.

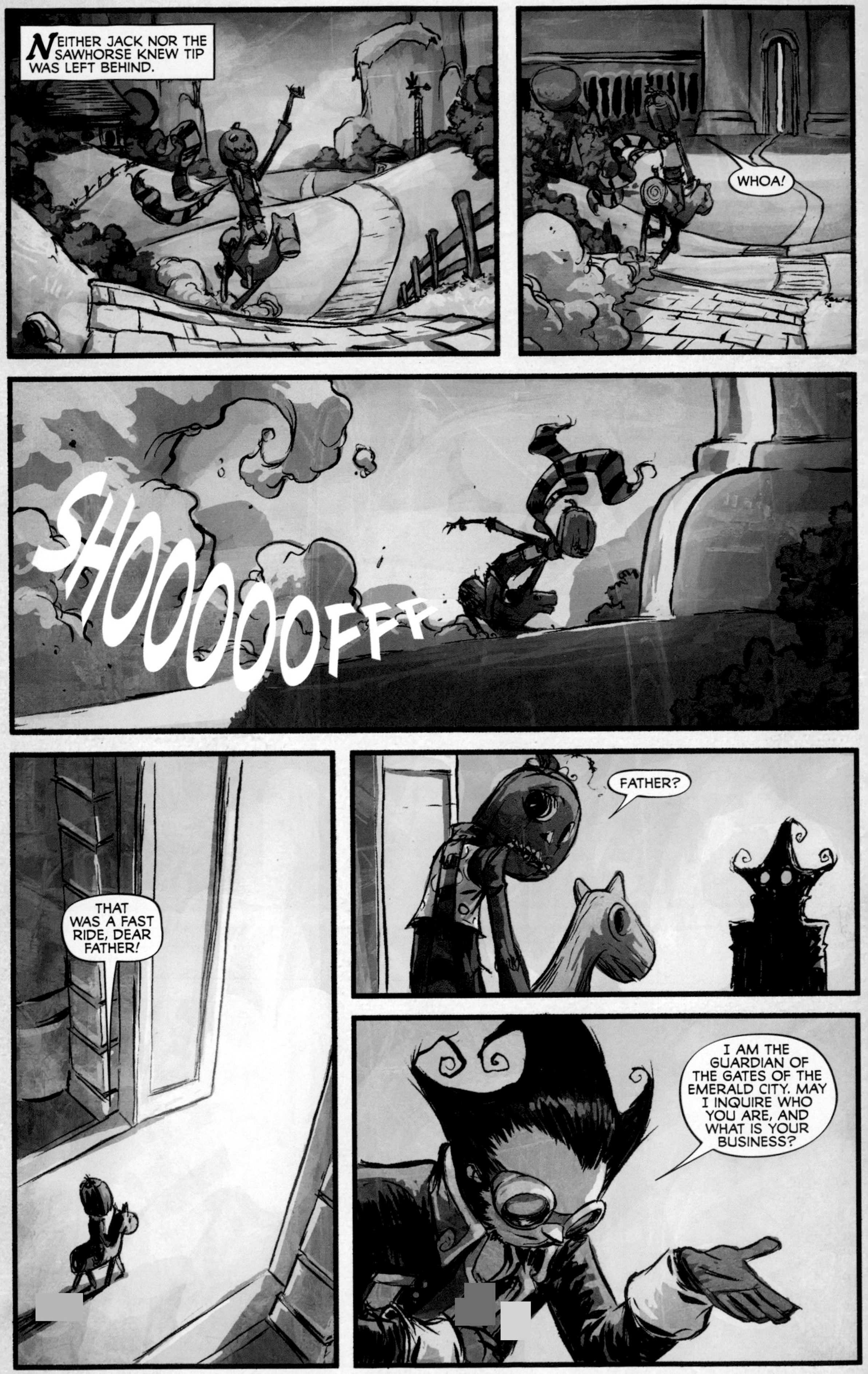
NEITHER JACK NOR THE SAWHORSE KNEW TIP WAS LEFT BEHIND.
WHOA!
SHOOOOOFFF
THAT WAS A FAST RIDE, DEAR FATHER!
FATHER?
I AM THE GUARDIAN OF THE GATES OF THE EMERALD CITY. MAY I INQUIRE WHO YOU ARE, AND WHAT IS YOUR BUSINESS?

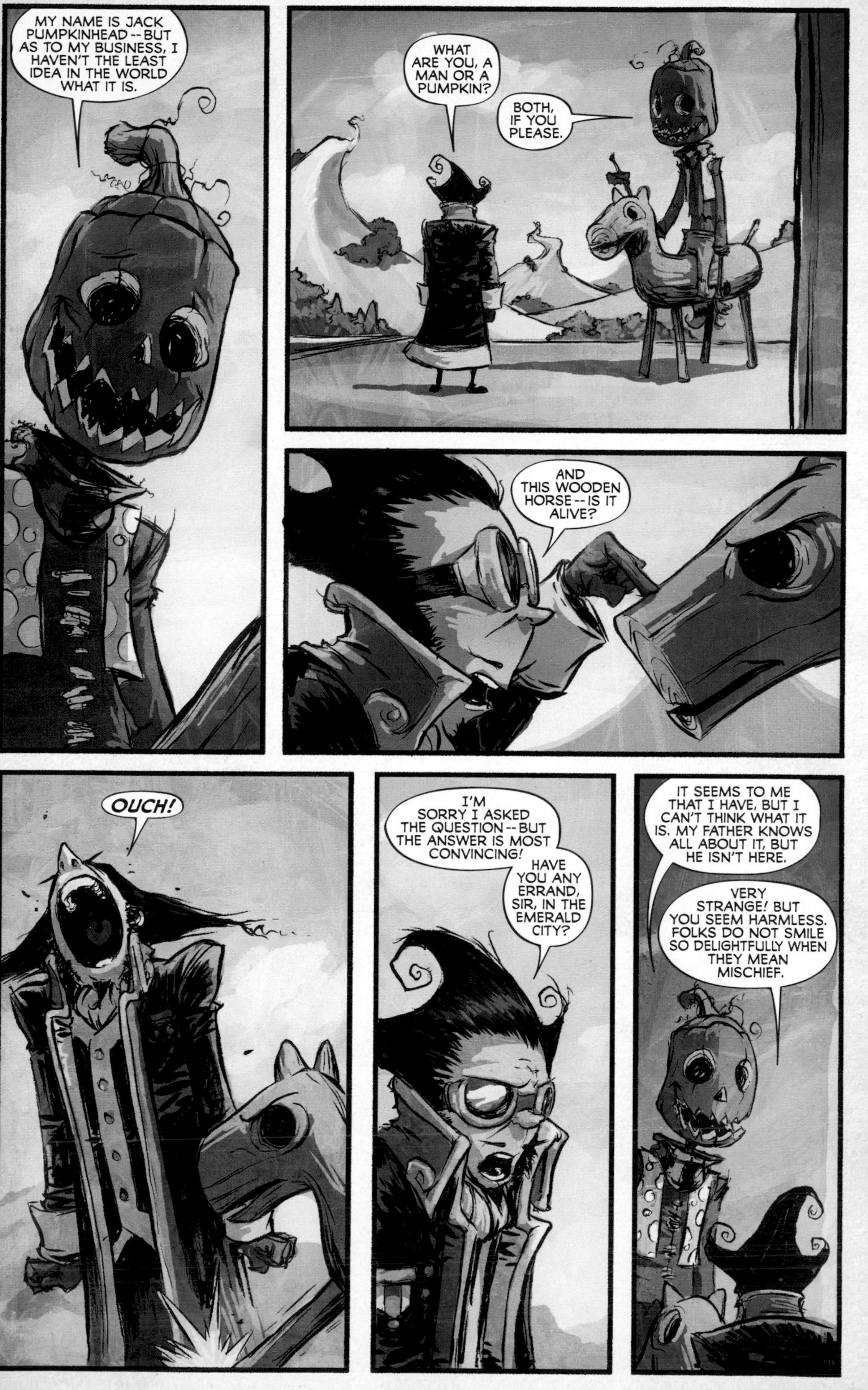
MY NAME IS JACK PUMPKINHEAD -- BUT AS TO MY BUSINESS, I HAVEN'T THE LEAST IDEA IN THE WORLD WHAT IT IS.
WHAT ARE YOU, A MAN OR A PUMPKIN?
BOTH, IF YOU PLEASE.
AND THIS WOODEN HORSE -- IS IT ALIVE?
OUCH!
I'M SORRY I ASKED THE QUESTION -- BUT THE ANSWER IS MOST CONVINCING!
HAVE YOU ANY ERRAND, SIR, IN THE EMERALD CITY?
IT SEEMS TO ME THAT I HAVE, BUT I CAN'T THINK WHAT IT IS. MY FATHER KNOWS ALL ABOUT IT, BUT HE ISN'T HERE.
VERY STRANGE! BUT YOU SEEM HARMLESS. FOLKS DO NOT SMILE SO DELIGHTFULLY WHEN THEY MEAN MISCHIEF.

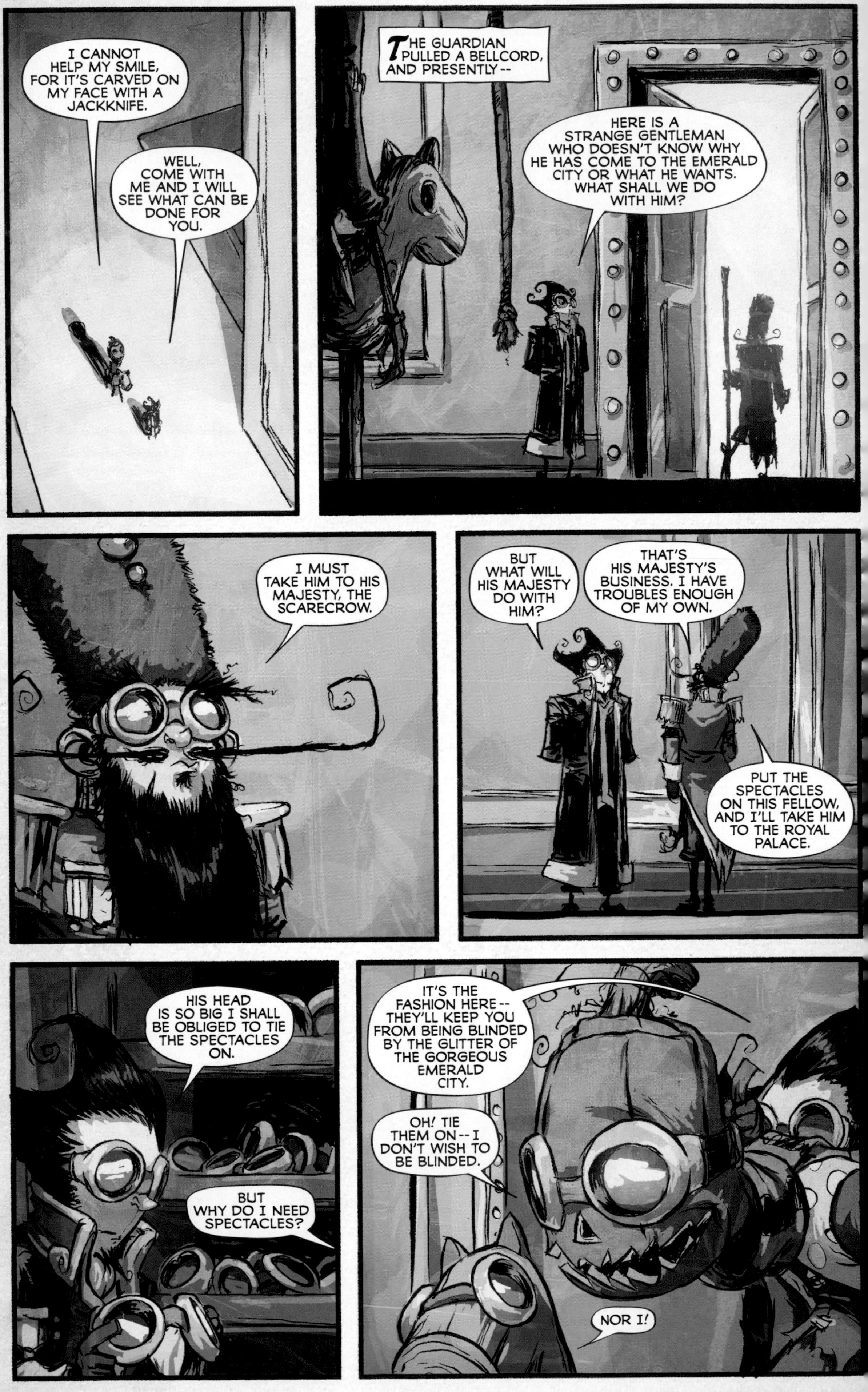
I CANNOT HELP MY SMILE, FOR IT'S CARVED ON MY FACE WITH A JACKKNIFE.
WELL, COME WITH ME AND I WILL SEE WHAT CAN BE DONE FOR YOU.
THE GUARDIAN PULLED A BELLCORD, AND PRESENTLY --
HERE IS A STRANGE GENTLEMAN WHO DOESN'T KNOW WHY HE HAS COME TO THE EMERALD CITY OR WHAT HE WANTS. WHAT SHALL WE DO WITH HIM?
I MUST TAKE HIM TO HIS MAJESTY, THE SCARECROW.
BUT WHAT WILL HIS MAJESTY DO WITH HIM?
THAT'S HIS MAJESTY'S BUSINESS. I HAVE TROUBLES ENOUGH OF MY OWN.
PUT THE SPECTACLES ON THIS FELLOW, AND I'LL TAKE HIM TO THE ROYAL PALACE.
HIS HEAD IS SO BIG I SHALL BE OBLIGED TO TIE THE SPECTACLES ON.
BUT WHY DO I NEED SPECTACLES?
IT'S THE FASHION HERE -- THEY'LL KEEP YOU FROM BEING BLINDED BY THE GLITTER OF THE GORGEOUS EMERALD CITY.
OH! TIE THEM ON -- I DON'T WISH TO BE BLINDED.
NOR I!

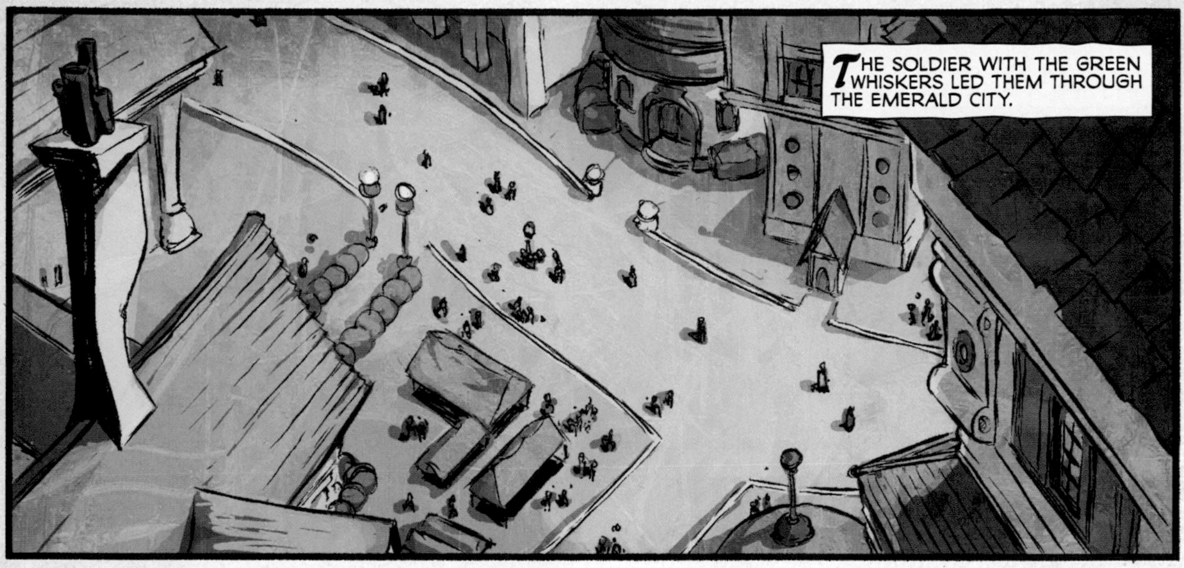
THE SOLDIER WITH THE GREEN WHISKERS LED THEM THROUGH THE EMERALD CITY.

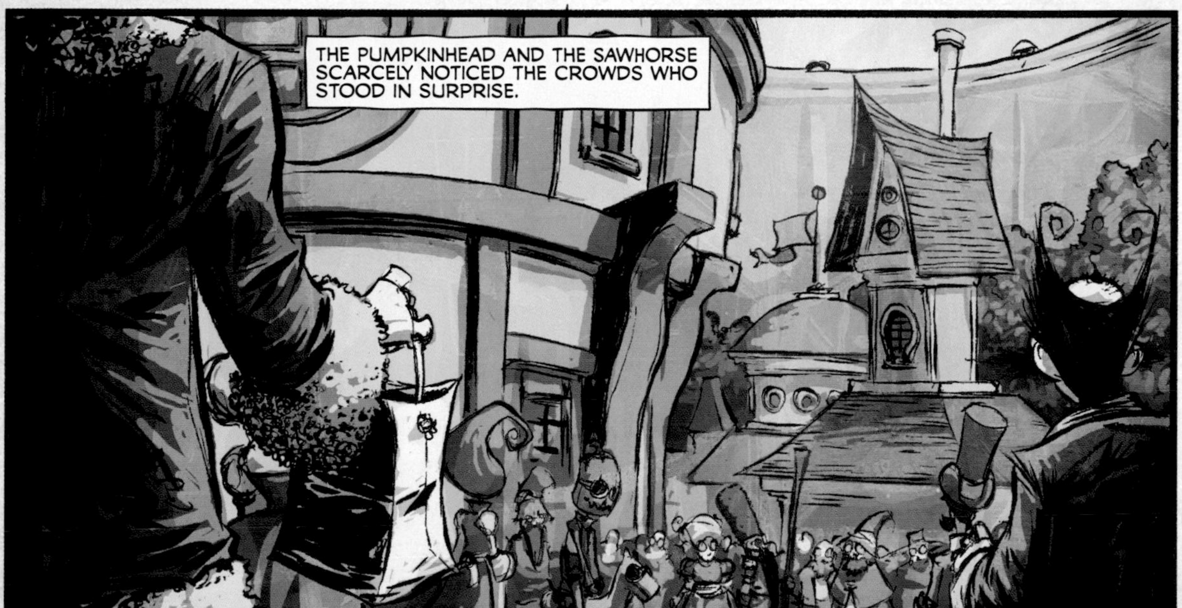
THE PUMPKINHEAD AND THE SAWHORSE SCARCELY NOTICED THE CROWDS WHO STOOD IN SURPRISE.

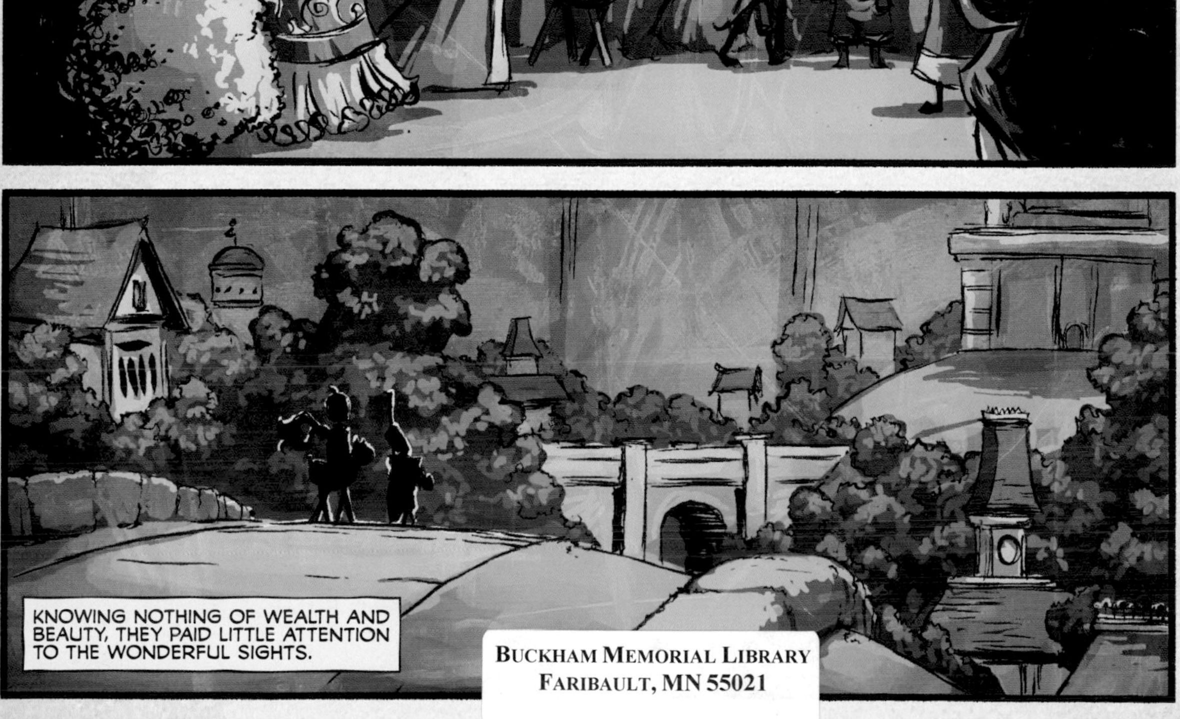
KNOWING NOTHING OF WEALTH AND BEAUTY, THEY PAID LITTLE ATTENTION TO THE WONDERFUL SIGHTS.

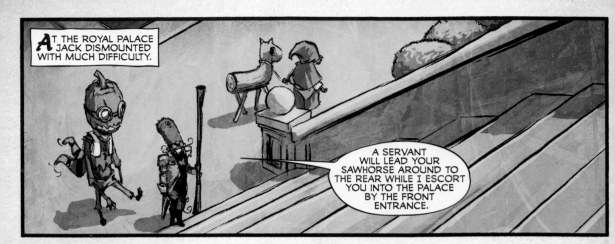

AT THE ROYAL PALACE JACK DISMOUNTED WITH MUCH DIFFICULTY.

A SERVANT WILL LEAD YOUR SAWHORSE AROUND TO THE REAR WHILE I ESCORT YOU INTO THE PALACE BY THE FRONT ENTRANCE.

JACK WAS LEFT IN A WAITING-ROOM WHILE THE SOLDIER WENT TO ANNOUNCE HIM.

IT SO HAPPENS THAT AT THIS HOUR HIS MAJESTY IS AT LEISURE AND GREATLY BORED FOR WANT OF SOMETHING TO DO, SO HE ORDERS HIS VISITOR TO BE SHOWN AT ONCE INTO HIS THRONE ROOM.

JACK FELT NO FEAR AT MEETING THE RULER OF THIS MAGNIFICENT CITY, BUT HE WAS MORE SURPRISED AT THE STRANGE APPEARANCE OF THIS REMARKABLE KING THAN BY ANY OTHER EXPERIENCE OF HIS BRIEF LIFE.

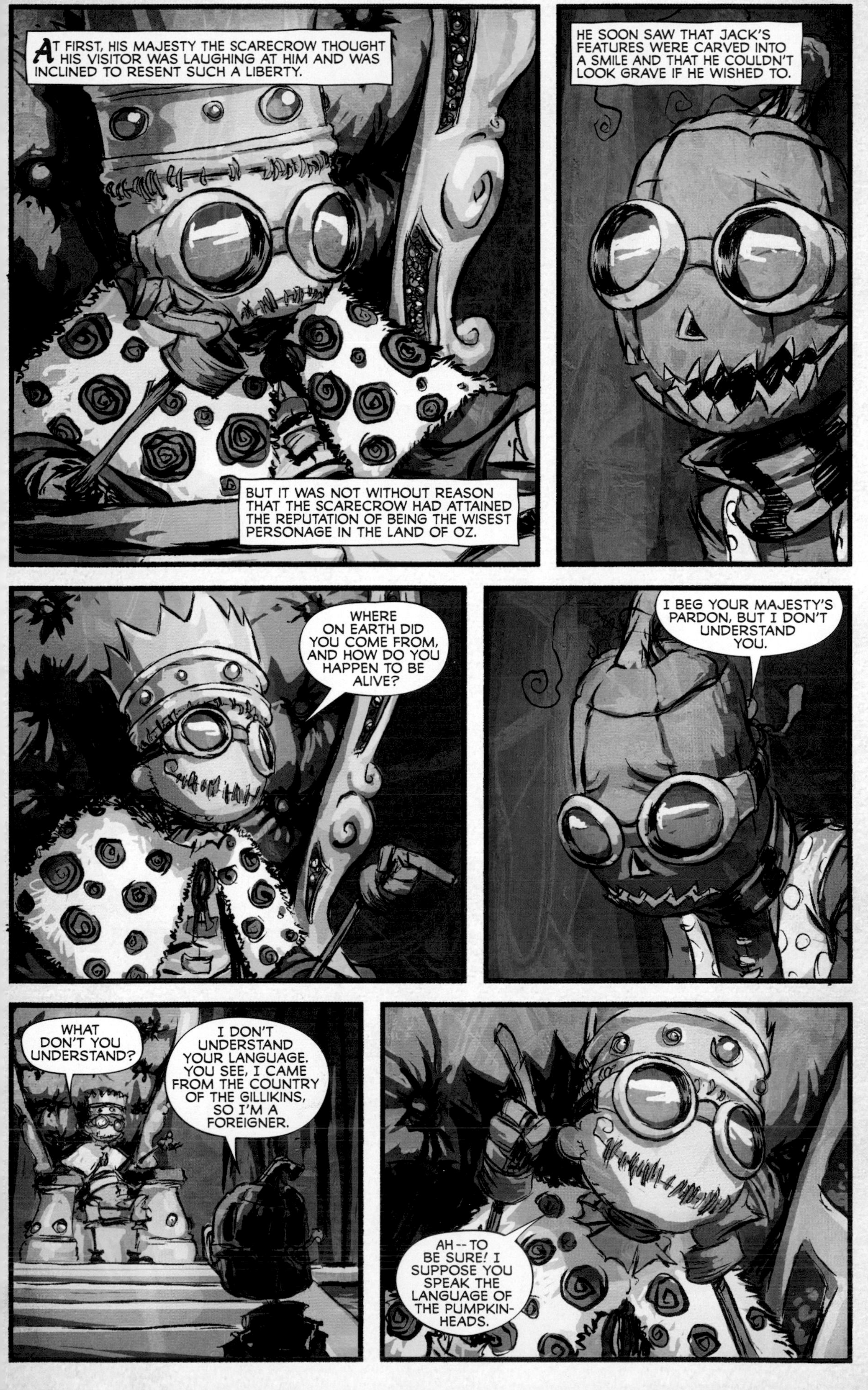
AT FIRST, HIS MAJESTY THE SCARECROW THOUGHT HIS VISITOR WAS LAUGHING AT HIM AND WAS INCLINED TO RESENT SUCH A LIBERTY.
BUT IT WAS NOT WITHOUT REASON THAT THE SCARECROW HAD ATTAINED THE REPUTATION OF BEING THE WISEST PERSONAGE IN THE LAND OF OZ.
HE SOON SAW THAT JACK'S FEATURES WERE CARVED INTO A SMILE AND THAT HE COULDN'T LOOK GRAVE IF HE WISHED TO.
WHERE ON EARTH DID YOU COME FROM, AND HOW DO YOU HAPPEN TO BE ALIVE?
I BEG YOUR MAJESTY'S PARDON, BUT I DON'T UNDERSTAND YOU.
WHAT DON'T YOU UNDERSTAND?
I DON'T UNDERSTAND YOUR LANGUAGE. YOU SEE, I CAME FROM THE COUNTRY OF THE GILLIKINS, SO I'M A FOREIGNER.
AH -- TO BE SURE! I SUPPOSE YOU SPEAK THE LANGUAGE OF THE PUMPKIN-HEADS.

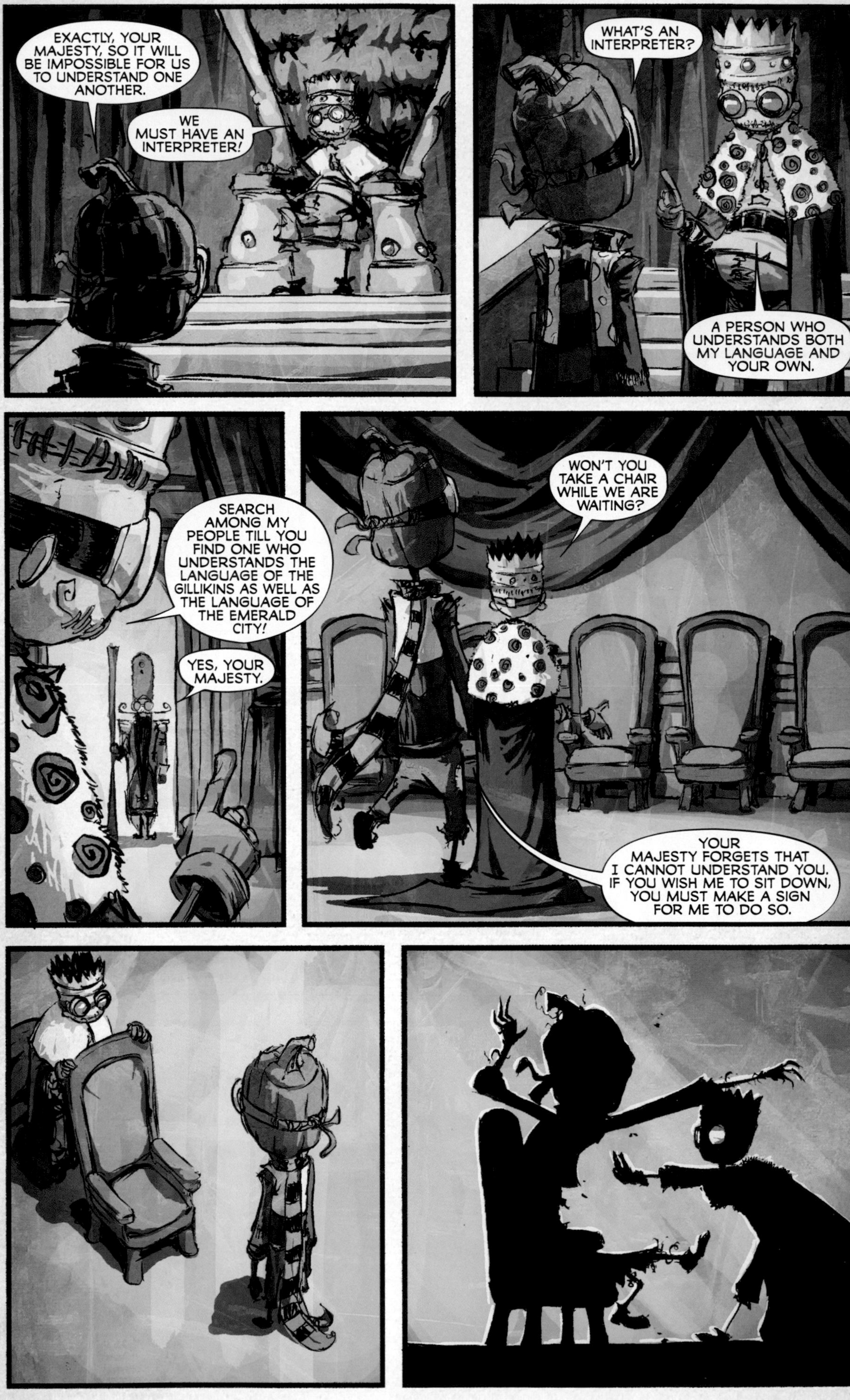
EXACTLY, YOUR MAJESTY, SO IT WILL BE IMPOSSIBLE FOR US TO UNDERSTAND ONE ANOTHER.
WE MUST HAVE AN INTERPRETER!
WHAT'S AN INTERPRETER?
A PERSON WHO UNDERSTANDS BOTH MY LANGUAGE AND YOUR OWN.
SEARCH AMONG MY PEOPLE TILL YOU FIND ONE WHO UNDERSTANDS THE LANGUAGE OF THE GILLIKINS AS WELL AS THE LANGUAGE OF THE EMERALD CITY!
YES, YOUR MAJESTY.
WON'T YOU TAKE A CHAIR WHILE WE ARE WAITING?
YOUR MAJESTY FORGETS THAT I CANNOT UNDERSTAND YOU. IF YOU WISH ME TO SIT DOWN, YOU MUST MAKE A SIGN FOR ME TO DO SO.

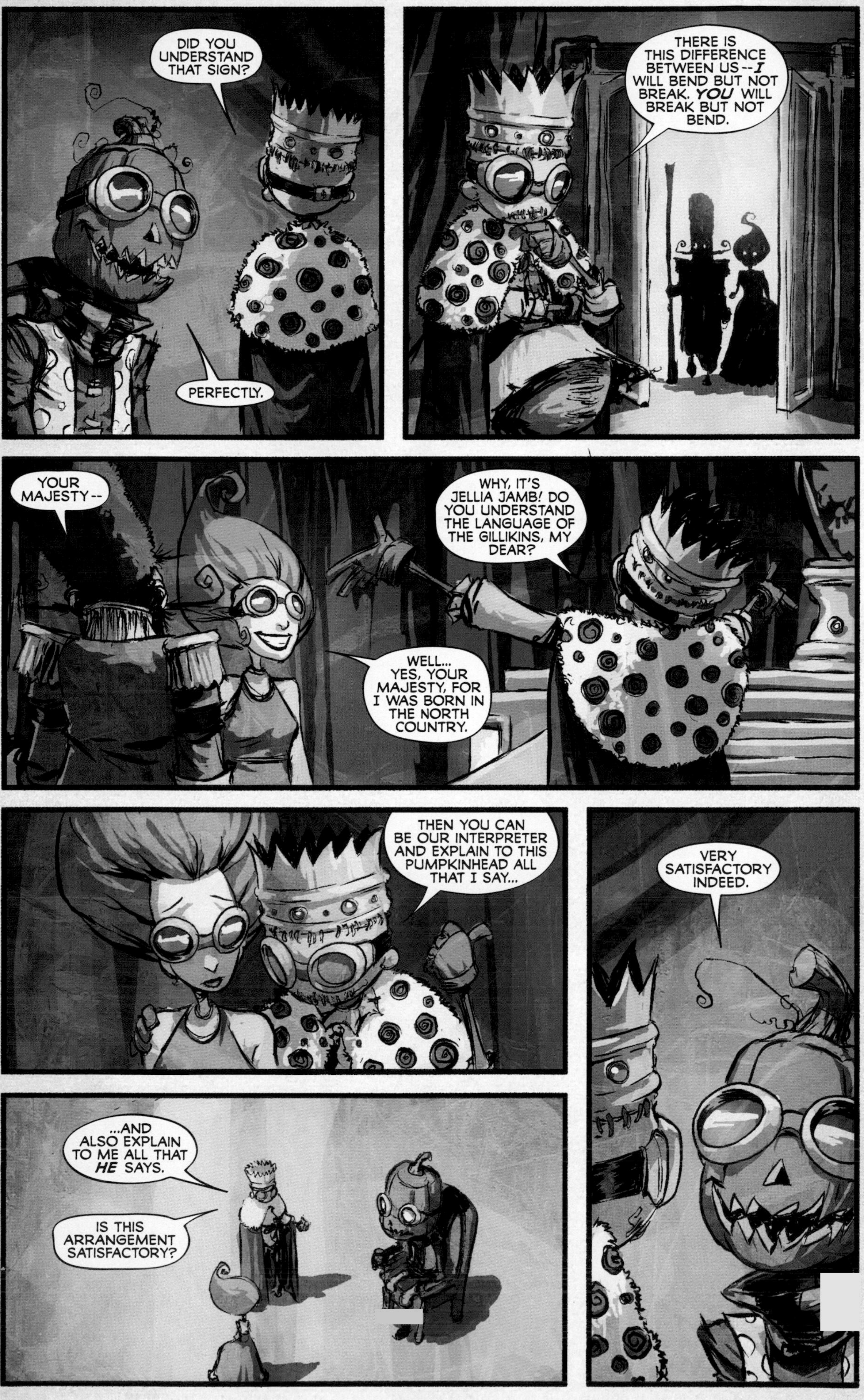
DID YOU UNDERSTAND THAT SIGN?
PERFECTLY.
THERE IS THIS DIFFERENCE BETWEEN US -- *I* WILL BEND BUT NOT BREAK. ***YOU*** WILL BREAK BUT NOT BEND.
YOUR MAJESTY --
WHY, IT'S JELLIA JAMB! DO YOU UNDERSTAND THE LANGUAGE OF THE GILLIKINS, MY DEAR?
WELL... YES, YOUR MAJESTY, FOR I WAS BORN IN THE NORTH COUNTRY.
THEN YOU CAN BE OUR INTERPRETER AND EXPLAIN TO THIS PUMPKINHEAD ALL THAT I SAY...
...AND ALSO EXPLAIN TO ME ALL THAT ***HE*** SAYS.
IS THIS ARRANGEMENT SATISFACTORY?
VERY SATISFACTORY INDEED.

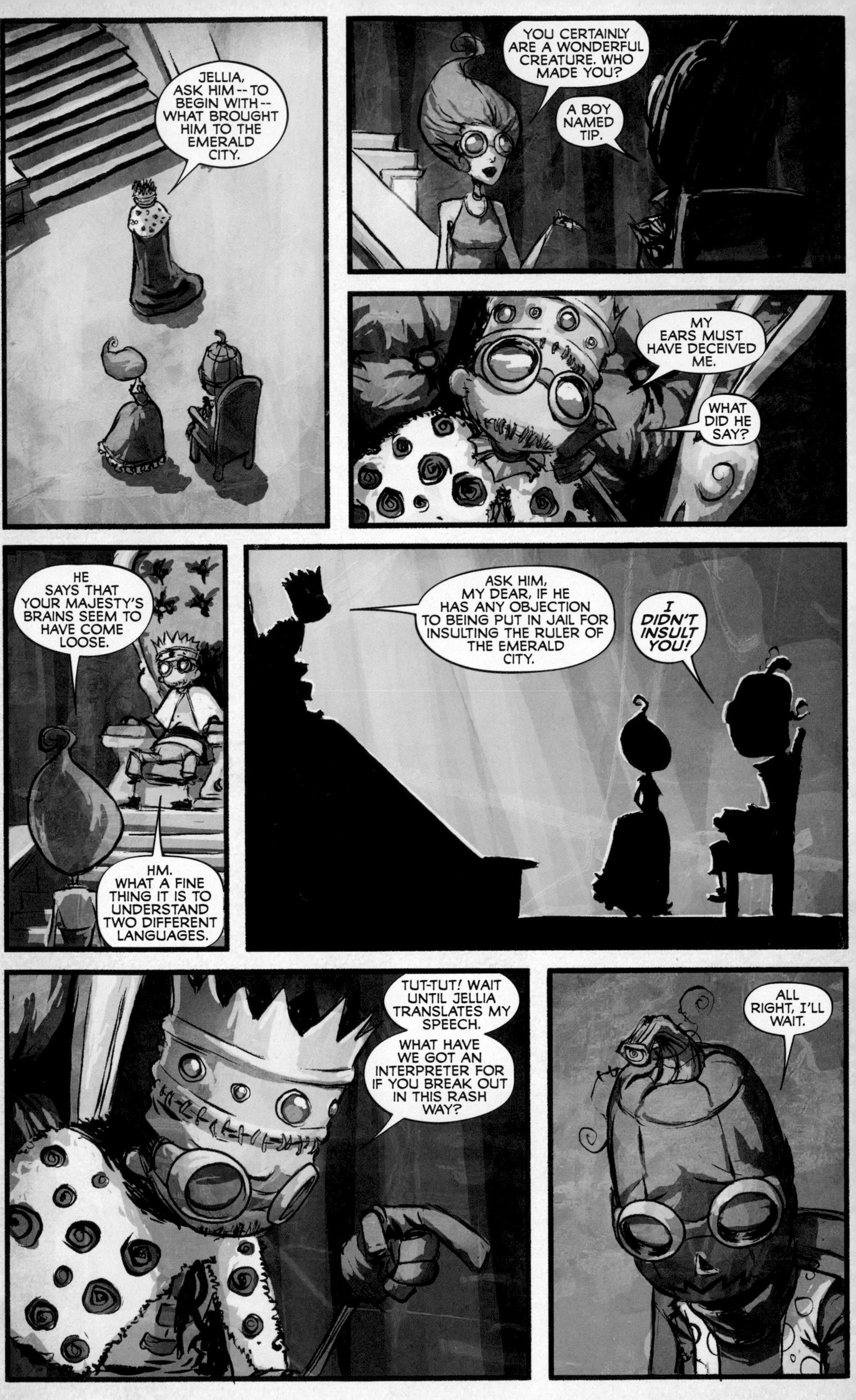
JELLIA, ASK HIM -- TO BEGIN WITH -- WHAT BROUGHT HIM TO THE EMERALD CITY.
YOU CERTAINLY ARE A WONDERFUL CREATURE. WHO MADE YOU?
A BOY NAMED TIP.
MY EARS MUST HAVE DECEIVED ME.
WHAT DID HE SAY?
HE SAYS THAT YOUR MAJESTY'S BRAINS SEEM TO HAVE COME LOOSE.
HM. WHAT A FINE THING IT IS TO UNDERSTAND TWO DIFFERENT LANGUAGES.
ASK HIM, MY DEAR, IF HE HAS ANY OBJECTION TO BEING PUT IN JAIL FOR INSULTING THE RULER OF THE EMERALD CITY.
I DIDN'T INSULT YOU!
TUT-TUT! WAIT UNTIL JELLIA TRANSLATES MY SPEECH.
WHAT HAVE WE GOT AN INTERPRETER FOR IF YOU BREAK OUT IN THIS RASH WAY?
ALL RIGHT, I'LL WAIT.

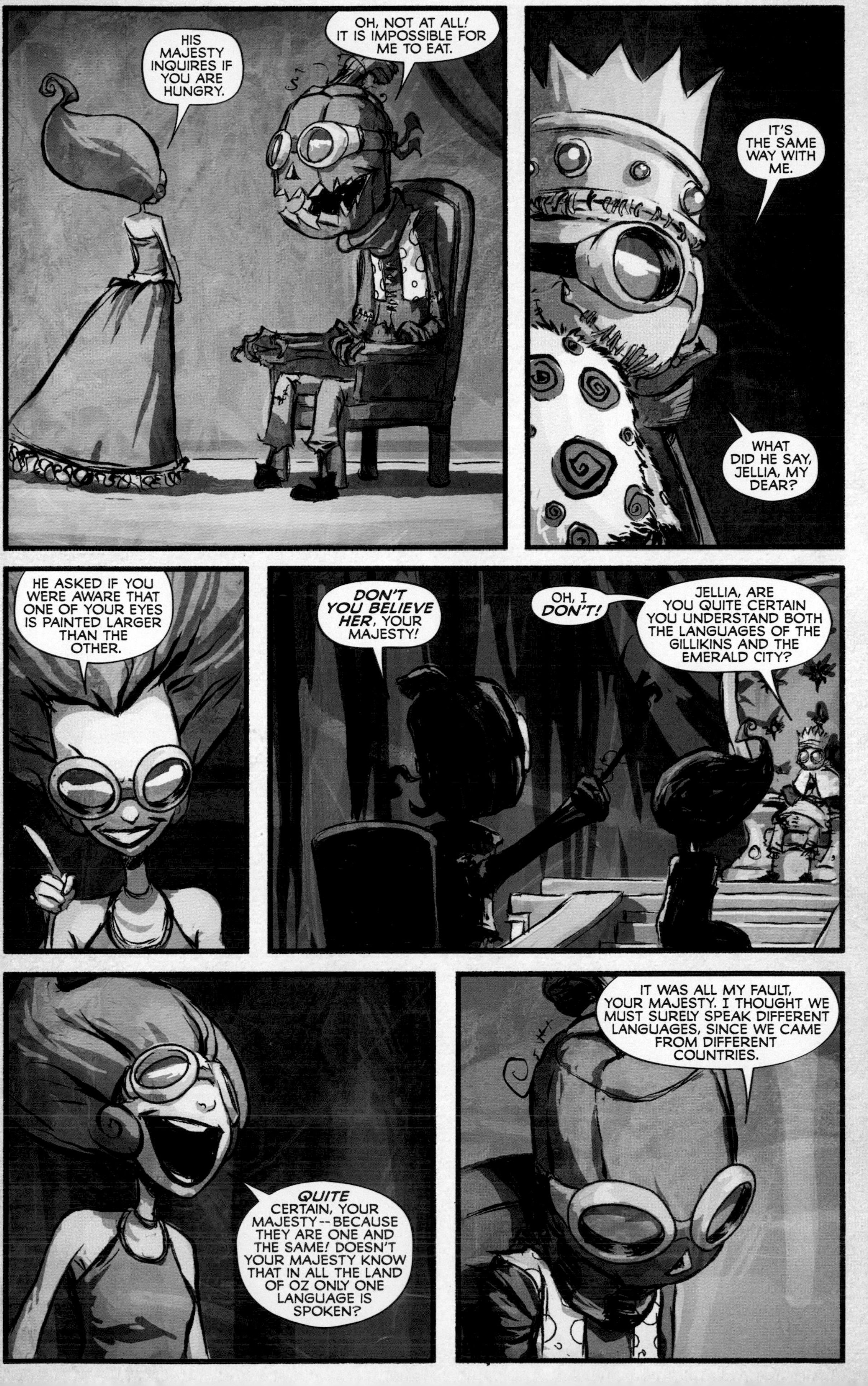

HIS MAJESTY INQUIRES IF YOU ARE HUNGRY.
OH, NOT AT ALL! IT IS IMPOSSIBLE FOR ME TO EAT.
IT'S THE SAME WAY WITH ME.
WHAT DID HE SAY, JELLIA, MY DEAR?
HE ASKED IF YOU WERE AWARE THAT ONE OF YOUR EYES IS PAINTED LARGER THAN THE OTHER.
DON'T YOU BELIEVE HER, YOUR MAJESTY!
OH, I DON'T!
JELLIA, ARE YOU QUITE CERTAIN YOU UNDERSTAND BOTH THE LANGUAGES OF THE GILLIKINS AND THE EMERALD CITY?
QUITE CERTAIN, YOUR MAJESTY--BECAUSE THEY ARE ONE AND THE SAME! DOESN'T YOUR MAJESTY KNOW THAT IN ALL THE LAND OF OZ ONLY ONE LANGUAGE IS SPOKEN?
IT WAS ALL MY FAULT, YOUR MAJESTY. I THOUGHT WE MUST SURELY SPEAK DIFFERENT LANGUAGES, SINCE WE CAME FROM DIFFERENT COUNTRIES.

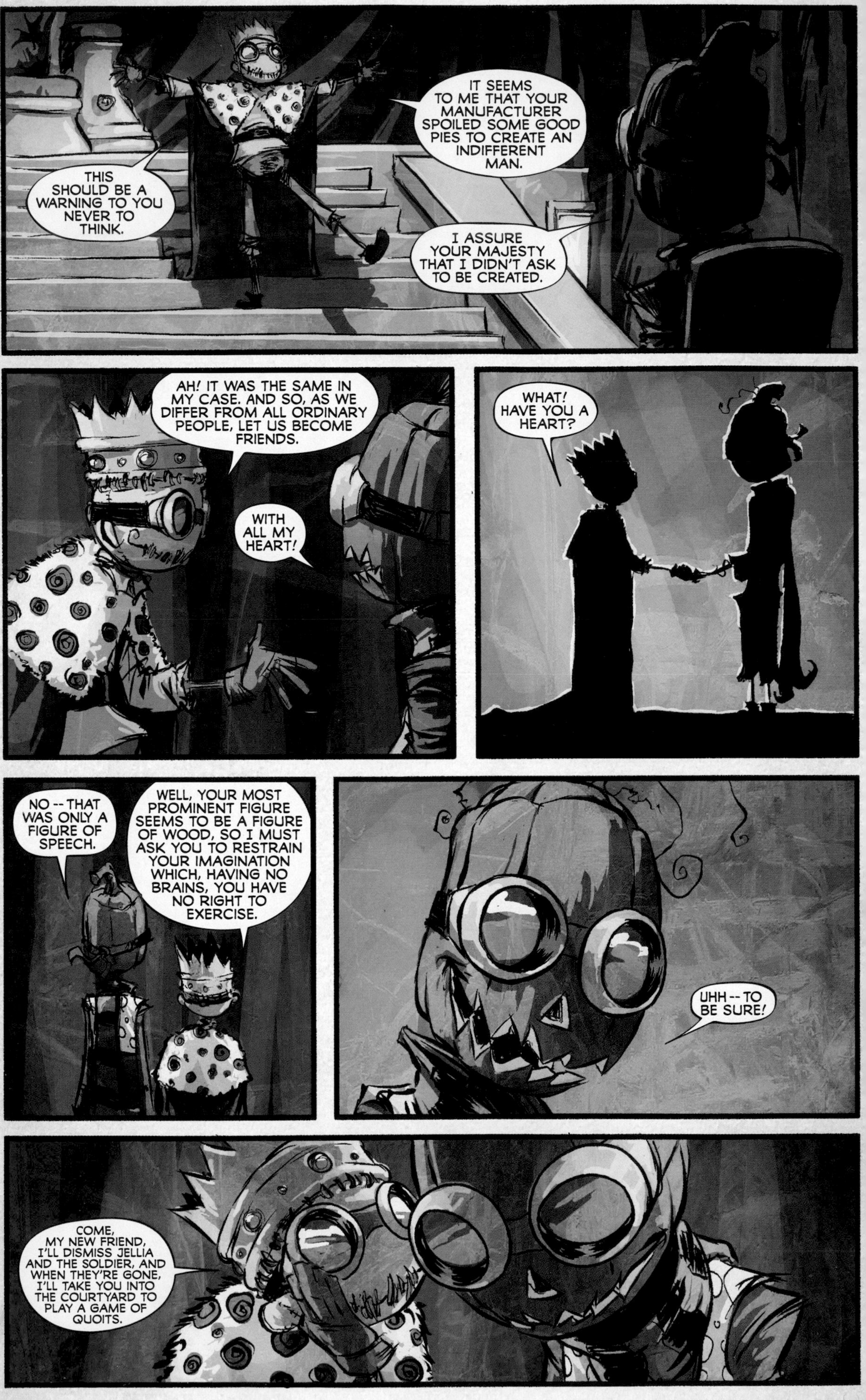
IT SEEMS TO ME THAT YOUR MANUFACTURER SPOILED SOME GOOD PIES TO CREATE AN INDIFFERENT MAN.
THIS SHOULD BE A WARNING TO YOU NEVER TO THINK.
I ASSURE YOUR MAJESTY THAT I DIDN'T ASK TO BE CREATED.
AH! IT WAS THE SAME IN MY CASE. AND SO, AS WE DIFFER FROM ALL ORDINARY PEOPLE, LET US BECOME FRIENDS.
WITH ALL MY HEART!
WHAT! HAVE YOU A HEART?
NO -- THAT WAS ONLY A FIGURE OF SPEECH.
WELL, YOUR MOST PROMINENT FIGURE SEEMS TO BE A FIGURE OF WOOD, SO I MUST ASK YOU TO RESTRAIN YOUR IMAGINATION WHICH, HAVING NO BRAINS, YOU HAVE NO RIGHT TO EXERCISE.
UHH -- TO BE SURE!
COME, MY NEW FRIEND, I'LL DISMISS JELLIA AND THE SOLDIER, AND WHEN THEY'RE GONE, I'LL TAKE YOU INTO THE COURTYARD TO PLAY A GAME OF QUOITS.